D0589182

Cyberspace Warrior

DAVID ORME

Ransom

13

Cyberspace Warrior
by David Orme
Illustrated by Jorge Mongiovi and Ulises Carpintero
Cover photographs: © Andreas Guskos and Robert Kohlhuber

Published by Ransom Publishing Ltd.
Radley House, 8 St. Cross Road, Winchester, Hampshire SO23 9HX
www.ransom.co.uk

ISBN   978 184167 451 3

First published in 2011

Originally published in 1998 by Stanley Thornes Publishers Ltd.

A CIP catalogue record of this book is available from the British Library.

Printed and bound in India by Nutech Print Services

CONTENTS

4

CYBERWORLD

Eddy Barnes stopped outside the door. CYBERWORLD it said, in big letters. This was the place!

Eddy went in. A woman was sitting at a desk.

'Good morning,' she said. 'My name's Danni. Welcome to Cyberworld!'

Cyberworld was the latest craze. You put on a special helmet. It linked up with your brain.

You could visit all sorts of worlds and have adventures. It was just as if you were there.

Danni showed Eddy the programs he could choose.

'Cyberspace warrior,' said Eddy. 'That looks good.'

'Become a warrior in Cyberspace.' it said. 'Defeat all the deadly enemies!'

There were pictures of some of the enemies. One was an alien with three heads. Another was a caveman with a big club of wood. The club had nails sticking out of it.

'That will be twenty pounds, please,' said Danni.

'Twenty pounds!' said Eddy. 'What a rip off!'

He paid the money anyway, and Danni took him into a small room. He sat in a chair.

'You can end the game at any time,' said Danni. 'All you have to do is shout out your

password. Whatever you do, don't forget your password!'

She put the helmet on his head.

'What password would you like?'

'I know,' said Eddy. 'This place is a real rip off. I'll choose RIP OFF as my password!'

Danni laughed. She pressed a switch.

'GAME ON,' said a voice.

NOT FOR THE PUBLIC TO KNOW
TOP SECRET
ZONE 13 FILES ONLY

THE GAME STARTS

Eddy found himself sitting on a big rock. He looked around. What a terrible place! There was nothing growing there. There were huge rocks scattered about. The sun was very hot.

He looked down at himself. He was wearing a leather skirt. He had a heavy leather jacket. A sword hung at his side.

Eddy didn't feel brave any more. He knew he would have to fight with a terrible enemy.

He was no good at fighting. He was a bit of a weed really. He didn't want to play any more.

Eddy knew that the game would stop if he shouted out the password. Now, what was that password again?

Suddenly, there was a roar. A huge man jumped out from behind a rock. He was dressed like Eddy. He had a sword.

Eddy was very frightened. When Eddy got frightened, he forgot things.

Eddy forgot the password.

He jumped up and started to run.

'Come here, you coward!' roared the warrior. 'Fight, you worm!'

Eddy was trying to remember the password. Perhaps it was what the other kids called him at school.

'Stupid weed!' he shouted.

This wasn't the password. But it made the big man very angry.

'What did you call me?' he yelled. 'Just you wait until I get you!'

Eddy tried to hide behind a rock. The big man saw him. Eddy was trapped!

'I'll chop you into little pieces!' roared the warrior. 'Now, which bit shall I chop off first?'

The huge sword started to chop. Suddenly, the big man disappeared. Eddy heard a voice.

'Round one is over. You lost. Get ready for round two!'

Eddy groaned. If only he could remember the password!

THE NEXT ROUND

Eddy was on an alien planet. There were three moons in the sky. He was in a forest of funny-looking trees. He remembered the alien in the picture. It had three heads, and you had to shoot all of them to kill the alien. He decided to hide in the trees.

Eddy checked for weapons. That must be a ray gun. That could be useful!

Eddy felt something tickling the back of his neck. He turned round.

Giant spiders! They were hanging down from the trees. They had huge webs. Eddy hated spiders. He fired the gun at them. Zap! Zap! Zap!

Eddy was not a good shot. At last, all the spiders were dead.

There was a roaring noise behind him. Eddy groaned. 'Why do all the enemies have to roar?' he wondered.

The three-headed alien was coming through the trees. It had a long slimy body and very short legs.

'Die, Earthman, die!' roared one of the heads.

Eddy aimed the gun. 'This ought to be easy!' he thought. He pulled the trigger.

Nothing happened.

He had used up the weapon on the spiders!

'Die, Earthman, die!' roared all three heads at once.

'Can't we talk about this?' asked Eddy.

If only he could remember the password.

He suddenly remembered the rude name he used for his little sister. Perhaps that was it!

'Slug face,' he yelled.

The alien heads screamed in rage.

'No one calls us slug face!' they yelled. 'Get ready to die. We will eat you alive! Now, which bit shall we eat first?'

The heads each chose a bit of Eddy to eat first. The teeth started to munch ...

'Round two is over. You lost. Get ready for round three!'

Whatever was that password?

TENTACLES OF DOOM!

Eddy found himself at the bottom of the sea. It was quite dark. He was wearing a mask. He had air tanks on his back.

Eddy didn't like it here. He thought he would swim to the surface.

Then he remembered he couldn't swim.

He tried kicking his legs. He didn't seem to be getting anywhere. He wondered what the enemy could be. He thought about great white sharks. He hoped it wasn't that! There was

only one thing he feared more than a great white shark. That was ...

A giant octopus!

Eddy knew the octopus was there when a tentacle grabbed his leg.

What weapon did he have? He reached down to his belt.

A knife! Good!

He looked at the knife. It was a bit small.

Not so good!

More tentacles grabbed Eddy. What was that password? It was something to do with how much money he had paid.

If only he hadn't gone to Cyberworld. Eddy was a real sucker.

'That's it!' thought Eddy.

'Sucker!' he shouted.

'You're right!' said the octopus. 'I forgot the suckers! Sorry about that!'

Suckers appeared on the tentacles. They held him tightly. Eddy couldn't reach the knife.

Suddenly, Eddy couldn't breathe. The octopus had pulled off his air tanks with its suckers!

Eddy struggled. Everything started to go black.

'Round three is over. You lost again. Not very good, are you? Prepare for round four!'

THE MUTANT KILLER ROBOT

Eddy was standing in a huge city. It looked very modern. He was wearing a silver uniform. A voice spoke in his ear.

'Calling all cops! Calling all cops! Mutant killer robot on the loose! Heading for Street 29!'

Eddy looked at the sign on the wall. He could have guessed.

The sign said: Street 29.

The mutant killer robot marched up the street. It had big glass eyes. They looked at Eddy.

'You are a cop!' said the robot. 'Cops are the enemies of the robots! Get ready …'

'Yes, I know,' said Eddy. 'Get ready to die!'

'How did you know I was going to say that?'

'Just a lucky guess,' said Eddy.

Eddy was getting cross now. He wanted to get out of this stupid game. He still couldn't remember the password. He tried to get past the robot. The robot grabbed him and wouldn't let him go.

Eddy didn't often lose his temper. But he did now.

'Let go of me, you stupid tin can!' he yelled. 'Or I'll RIP OFF your arm!'

Suddenly the robot was gone. The city was gone as well. Eddy found himself back at Cyberworld.

'GAME OVER,' said the voice.

Danni seemed really impressed.

'You got to level four!' she said. 'You must be really tough. Most people give up when they see the octopus!'

Eddy felt proud. Really tough!

'Did you enjoy it?'

'It was great. As soon as I've saved another twenty pounds, I'll be back!'

About the Author

David Orme is an expert on strange, unexplained events. For his protection (and yours) we cannot show a photograph of him.

David created the Zone 13 files to record the cases he studied. Some of these files really do involve aliens, but many do not. Aliens are not everywhere. Just in most places.

These stories are all taken from the Zone 13 files. They will not be here for long. Read them while you can.

But don't close your eyes when you go to sleep at night. **They** will be watching you.